The
Boy Who Stuck
Out His Tongue

8-00

Dedicated to my father, Benjamin Roseman,
Hungarian-born spinner of tales — E. T.

For my sister, Pam — J. C. M.

Barefoot Books
37 West 17th Street
4th Floor East
New York, New York 10011

Text copyright © 2000 by Edith Tarbescu
Illustrations copyright © 2000 by Judith Christine Mills

The moral right of Edith Tarbescu to be identified as the author and
Judith Christine Mills to be identified as the illustrator of this work has been asserted

This book is printed on 100% acid-free paper

This book was typeset in Berling bold 20pt on 32pt leading
The illustrations were prepared in acrylic on medium thick illustration board

Graphic design by Design/Section, England
Color separation by Color Gallery, Malaysia
Printed and bound in Hong Kong by South China Printing Co. (1988) Ltd.

1 3 5 7 9 8 6 4 2

U.S. Cataloging-in-Publication Data (Library of Congress Standards)

Tarbescu, Edith.
    The boy who stuck out his tongue : a Yiddish folk tale / written by Edith
Tarbescu ; illustrated by Judith Christine Mills. —1st ed.
[32]p. : col. ill. ;   cm.
Summary: When the widow's son sticks out his tongue once too often, he finds
himself in trouble. But the kind-hearted folk of the little Hungarian village are
quick to rally around.
ISBN 1-84148-067-3
1. Yiddish literature. 2. Folk literature, Yiddish. I. Mills, Judith Christine, ill.
II. Title.
398.2 21 2000 AC CIP

The
Boy Who Stuck
Out His Tongue

A YIDDISH FOLK TALE

written by
EDITH TARBESCU

illustrated by
JUDITH CHRISTINE MILLS

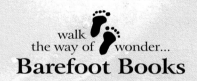

walk
the way of wonder...
Barefoot Books

Once, in a little Hungarian village, known for its kind but foolish folk, there was a great snowstorm.

When the peddler's widow called her only son indoors to light a fire in the stove, the boy answered, "Not now," and stuck out his tongue at his mother.

"But you promised me you'd light the fire. You even gave me your word."

"Promise, schmomise, I'm too busy." He packed another snowball and sent it flying.

"Wait till I get you," she shouted.

"Nah, nah, nah, you can't catch me!"

They ran around in circles, and just as his mother was about to grab him, he stuck out his tongue again. This time, he slipped and fell against a wrought-iron fence. It was so cold that his tongue stuck to a rail. When the woman saw what had happened, she tried to free her son, but she couldn't get him loose. So the poor widow trudged through the snow until she reached the shoemaker's shop.

After he heard what had happened, Mendel the cobbler shrugged. "I *wish* I could help," he said. "But what could I do?"

The woman pointed to the rows of shoes lining the shop. "You know about tongues."

Mendel explained, "Tongues in shoes, I know. Tongues in boots, I know. Tongues frozen on a fence — I don't know. Come, let's go and see Yussel the butcher."

"What can I get for you today?" asked Yussel, who was sitting on a low, wooden stool plucking chickens.

When the woman finished telling him her problem, Yussel shrugged. "If I could be of help, I would. But I never heard of such a thing."

She pointed to the meat in the window. "Look, you have all kinds of meat."

"Fresh meat, I know. Smoked meat, I know," said Yussel the butcher. "But I never met a frozen tongue, long or short. I wouldn't know one, even if it walked into my shop."

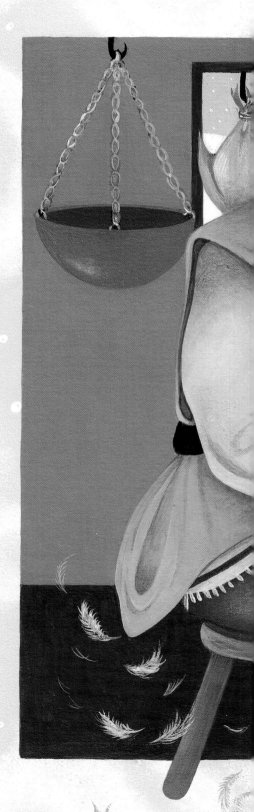

So they all went across the street to Hershel the baker. The baker said he had never heard of such a thing either, but he grabbed a bag of utensils and went along to help. When they got to the boy, Hershel emptied his little bag.

"A rolling pin, I can't use. Cookie cutters, I can't use. AHA..." He pulled out a small pouch filled with yeast and poured some on the boy's tongue. "When you want bread to rise, you add yeast," explained Hershel the baker. "So – his tongue should rise, too."

"It's a *great* idea," said Yussel the butcher.

"Brilliant idea!" said Mendel the shoemaker.

The woman looked from one to the other. Maybe it was true what people said; maybe this town was full of fools.

Meanwhile, a crowd was gathering, and everybody was arguing about what to do.

"I have an idea," said the cook, pulling a spatula out of his apron. "I've flipped pancakes; I've flipped eggs, so why not a tongue?"

The crowd moved closer, holding their breath as they watched every twist and turn of the cook's wrist.

Finally, the cook shook his head. "It's no use," he muttered. "A tongue is not like a pancake or an egg."

"That's *right*," shouted the crowd. "A tongue is not like a pancake or an egg."

"I have an idea," cried the carpenter. "We'll build a little hut around the boy. That way he'll stay warm till we find a way to set him free."

While the carpenter ran to fetch some wood, the cook arrived with a pot of chicken soup. Then the baker returned with pretzels piled high on a plate, and somebody set up a folding table.

When the carpenter returned, the townspeople began cutting and sawing, happy to be helping. When the boy saw how much his neighbors cared about him, he remembered how often he had refused to help them. And he started crying.

"Don't cry," they told him. "We're here to help you."

Just then a traveling blacksmith happened to come along. When he heard what the problem was, he collected hot coals from the nearest fireplace and piled them around the iron rail.

"The coals will warm the iron, the iron will melt the ice, and the boy will be free," said the blacksmith. Then he sat near the rail and fanned the coals.

The boy couldn't believe what he had heard. He was also getting hungry. He closed his eyes and imagined plates full of potato pancakes with applesauce. He tried to speak, but the only sound he could make was "Ahhhhh!"

While the blacksmith waited, the people came to see if the ice was melting and to touch the fence. The heat started rising; the rail was finally warming up. Even the boy's face became flushed. Finally, the blacksmith said, "Try wiggling your tongue."

The boy tried, but nothing happened. He tried again. And again, until he felt his tongue wiggle a bit.

"Look," the boy's mother shouted. "He's free!"

The boy hugged his mother and spun her around. "I'm sorry I was naughty," he told her. "I'll never do it again."

After that, he thanked the blacksmith and said to the people, "I promise to help you whenever you need it."

And from then on, he helped the baker knead bread, the cobbler lace boots, the carpenter build houses, and the butcher pluck chickens.

And the people of the little village learned something, too. They learned how to free a frozen tongue.

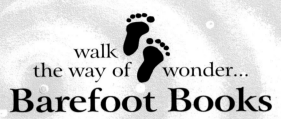

walk
the way of wonder...
Barefoot Books

The barefoot child symbolizes the human being who is in harmony
with the natural world and moves freely across boundaries of many kinds.
Barefoot Books explores this image with a range of high-quality picture books
for children of all ages. We work with artists, writers, and storytellers from
many cultures, focusing on themes that encourage independence of spirit,
promote understanding and acceptance of different traditions,
and foster a lifelong love of learning.
www.barefoot-books.com